THE ELDEST
By Nona

Published by Nona Gallery
Printed in the United Kingdom
First Paperback Edition 2022

ISBN - 978-1-7397827-1-9

@nonaGalleryArt
www.nonaGallery.com

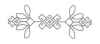

CONTENTS

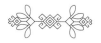

PREFACE

Thirty-one hand-drawn traditional ink illustrations in thirty-one days. An annual challenge set on the internet known as Inktober, a challenge I had attempted and spectacularly failed first time around. Lessons were learnt from past mistakes, and a plan was laid out for my second attempt at the challenge. This time around I created an incentive to not give up. I would have each drawing be part of a story, therefore I had to finish the full Inktober challenge if I wanted to conclude the story. Did I succeed? Technically no. I took much longer than thirty-one days, however, I did complete thirty-one traditional drawings, which you are about to see in this book.

I originally planned on creating this story to challenge myself, and to hopefully improve my abilities as an artist. As well as to learn how to create a storybook from start to finish. However, I also really wanted to share with others this lesser-known folktale, which I loved so much growing up. It tackles the darkest of subjects, death, and although it could quite easily be seen as a very morbid tale, I personally always interpreted it as showing how death isn't something to fear, instead, it should be welcomed as a part of life. Whatever way you choose to interpret the story yourself, I hope you enjoy my retelling and the images I created to accompany the story.

THE ELDEST

Far away in a country where the forests are ancient and dark, and the rivers are wide and gentle, there lived two young sisters. The two sisters did absolutely everything together, inseparable they lived a happy and playful life. But they couldn't stay children forever and as the sisters grew in age they also grew distant from each other. Like with all things time made them change from what they were to who they needed to become, despite their strong sisterly bond, gradually each became more independent from the other. For each had their own destiny.

The youngest of the sisters was blessed with good fortune. She grew in beauty and grace, so much so that rumours spread of an enchantress that would steal the heart of anyone who looked upon her, and it wasn't long before the rumours proved true. As luck would have it, when a visiting Mahārāja from a neighbouring Kingdom curiously visited the Youngest Sister and laid eyes on her his heart was indeed stolen, but fortunately for them both, her heart was stolen too. For they both instantly fell deeply in love with each other. The Youngest Sister's good fortune had allowed her to find and marry her soulmate. However, this meant she had to leave her childhood home and venture abroad, where she was to become a beloved and kind Maharani. As there is a balance to the world and in order to live such a blessed life she had to leave her Eldest Sister behind and sacrifice their life together.

Now the eldest of the sisters was less fortunate, but never the less she grew up strong and filled with wisdom. Once she saw her Younger Sister happily leave to become a great ruler of a foreign land, she decided to also leave their childhood home and adventure out on her own. She enlisted in her Kingdom's army, and after several years of hard training and valiant exploits, she became a noble soldier. Succeding in many heroic crusades and conflicts. However, the many battles had left the Eldest Sister scarred and haunted. Haunted by three ghosts, the ghosts of guilt, regret, and grief. These ghosts endlessly tormented the Eldest Sister and with great despair, they eventually drove her to abandon her position in the army. With only three small ration packs and her sword in hand, she fled the army, her home, and her Younger Sister. But no matter how far she ran, she could not elude her ghosts.

hilst travelling, continuously attempting to retreat away from the world, she stumbled upon an old beggar woman. The woman suddenly clung to the Eldest Sister's feet pleading desperately with her to stop and listen to her plight and imploring her to donate some food as she was so starved. Despite her own torment by the ghosts, the Eldest Sister not only stopped to sit and listen to what the beggar had to say but also gave the beggar woman one of her ration packs. After a long while, the beggar woman finally finished telling her tale and eating her fill. So the Eldest Sister rose to her feet, bid farewell, and then continued on her quest to rid herself of her tormenting ghosts. However after such a long respite the Eldest Sister was now in such a hurry to continue on her journey that she didn't notice the beggar women remove her ghost of guilt, or that with this her shoulders became much lighter.

Continuing in her attempt to outrun the torment of her ghosts, the Eldest Sister travelled further into the unknown world to places not found yet on any map. After days of not seeing another soul, she suddenly spotted a short ageing beggar-man sat alone in the clearing of a forest. The old man said nothing, and did not stop the Eldest Sister, but how could she be so generous towards the beggar woman, and now ignore this man in a similar situation?

So she stopped to speak to the man, and then without being asked chose to give him her second ration pack. While he ate she sat beside him to keep him company and once he was contently done she bid him farewell. Then hurried on with her journey. She left so fast in fact that she did not notice him take away the ghost of regret that haunted her, or that with it her feet became more steadfast.

The Eldest Sister continued on her journey to escape her torment. When without warning a great monster appeared blocking her path. The monster roared and, in shock, the Eldest Sister quickly drew her sword, but this only enraged the beast. He growled menacingly, his rumble echoing through the air. Now in fear of her life, the Eldest Sister launched her assault. Upon lunging towards the great beast sword first the Eldest Sister was quick to realise that the creature did not attack back, instead, he was cowering in fear. Just as quickly as she had launched her attack she reacted to the creature's sudden timidness, stopping mid-strike.

Once her uncertainty of the situation faded she was able to reevaluate her surroundings, which allowed her to notice that the creature was in fact badly wounded. Suddenly his initial aggression towards her made complete sense, as the anger she thought she had seen in his eyes had just been fear. And just like her, this creature must have been running away from whatever had caused him such harm. Rather than slaying the beast, she gently calmed him gaining his trust, and then tenderly began treating his injuries.

Suddenly a great bellowing grumble came from the creature's stomach. He was hungry. But the Eldest Sister only had one ration pack remaining, and after days of endless travel, she too was in need of food. She could give away just half, but she had given the beggars a full ration pack each, and the creature deserved no less than them. So the Eldest Sister concluded that she would just make do without any and gave all of her rations away.

Tentatively leaning in to pass the ration pack to the creature she noticed his large clawed paw reach over to her side and carefully remove her ghost of grief and all that tethered it to her. And upon the ghost's release, it abruptly occurred to her that her other ghosts were gone too. After this unexpected realisation, there was a great explosion from where the creature stood, and the Eldest Sister was thrown backwards through the air.

From the smoke and dust of the explosion appeared a mighty wizard adorned in masks. They reassured the startled Eldest Sister and explained their deception. For they had been in disguise as the talkative beggar woman, the ageing beggar man, and the injured creature. And that during all meetings the Eldest Sister had proven herself truly noble and kind of heart. The wizard continued praising her and asked if there was anything she wished for. But the Eldest Sister explained that meeting the wizard alone in all their forms was good fortune enough and that they had already granted all that she wished by removing her ghosts of torment. Therefore there was nothing else that she needed. She also added that her actions weren't that extraordinary as they were only the right thing to do, and not worth so much praise.

The wizard dismissed the Eldest Sister's humble comments, stating that doing what is right can often be the hardest and most selfless decision, and decided that if she did not request anything they would instead gift her their playing cards and a burlap sack that they carried with them. Then as the wizard was about to disappear, a playful grin grew on their face and they reminded the Eldest Sister that there is a balance to the world. They predicted that the good fortune she had just received would mean misfortune would befall another. And for some mysterious reason, the Eldest Sister instantly thought of her Youngest Sister. Panicked and with an uneasy heart she made haste towards the kingdom her sister now ruled over. The wizard, with their all-knowing power, faded from sight until not even their mischievous grin remained.

Upon arriving at her Youngest Sister's kingdom the Eldest Sister was met with a grim atmosphere. She spotted a small group of gloomy women and when she approached them they didn't even lift their heads to look at her, as if the despair they carried on their shoulders weighed down their worn bones. Despite continuous appeals for information on what was happening in the kingdom, none of the women would speak, it was like they were afraid someone might overhear and punish them for their loose lips. All they would do was point the Eldest Sister in the direction of the Mahārāja.

With their direction, she hurried to the where her Youngest Sister and her husband, the Mahārāja, were currently sheltered and found them distressed and emotional. They, unlike the women outside in the street, were quick to confide in the Eldest Sister that the Kingdom had suddenly become ransacked with demons. Demons that didn't cease tormenting their citizens, destroying all crops, stealing valuables, and commandeering property, such as the royal palace where they had taken up residence. The Youngest Sister had been left unable to sleep due to concern for her people, the stress and exhaustion of this ordeal had begun to diminish her health, leaving her frail and pale-faced. Extremely worried for her Youngest Sister, and feeling that the current misfortune befalling the kingdom was all her fault, the Eldest Sister decided that she would head to the royal palace and do away with the demons herself.

The Youngest Sister begged her to reconsider, scared for her Eldest Sister's life. She explained that the kingdom's royal army had already attempted to defeat the demons, but not a single soldier had returned alive from the palace. But the Eldest Sister would not listen, as she was far more concerned with her Youngest Sister's life than her own. Unable to be stopped, she rushed straight to the royal palace.

At first, when the Eldest Sister arrived at the royal palace, although ransacked, the building appeared to be empty. Confused, the Eldest Sister scoured the palace halls looking for anyone or anything that may have caused all this damage. But it was to no avail, confused and uncertain she found her self in the palace's great hall, she slumped in a chair and wondered what she should do next. Suddenly she was startled by the chimes of the hall's grand clock as it struck midnight. Upon the twelfth chime, a great gust of wind swept through the rooms and halls, filling the palace with all types of demons.

These demons were quick to notice the Eldest Sister sat in the great hall, and with evil grins surrounded her in her chair and questioned why she had dared enter the palace alone. The Eldest Sister calmly replied that she had heard a rumour the demons enjoyed card games and gambling and wondered if they would partake in a few games with her, the only condition being that they must use her own set of cards. The demons were quick to accept this offer, excited to claim another victim and gain even more wealth.

Hours had passed and the evil grins on the demon's faces had all faded away. How was this possible? It didn't matter what game they played, or how much they cheated, the Eldest Sister always won. For little did they know the Eldest Sister was playing with the cards the wizard had gifted her. These cards were enchanted so no matter who or what she played she would always win. As dawn approached the demons realised that they had in their confusion and shock gambled away all the riches they had plundered from the kingdom, and now they had nothing left to gamble with. This enraged the demons, loud angry shrieks filled the great hall. They couldn't understand how the Eldest Sister had bested them, but they didn't care anymore. She had embarrassed them, so now she would have to pay with her life.

Enraged the demons surrounded the Eldest Sister. Menacingly they asked if she had any last words before they sent her to the depths of hell. But the Eldest Sister, unfazed by the sudden onslaught, calmly picked up her sack and asked the demons did they know what it was? The demons confused and irritated snapped back that it was just a sack. The Eldest Sister smirked and told the demons that if it was a sack, then they should get into it! And with that, every demon was swept off their feet and hurdled towards the sack.

It didn't matter what they clung to or how much they fought, the power of the sack was too great, and they were all forced inside. For you see the sack was one of the gifts from the wizard and, like the playing cards, was enchanted. Enchanted so that no matter who or what the Eldest Sister told to get inside they would be forced to oblige.

With the sack now filled with the demons that besieged the kingdom, the Eldest Sister quickly tied the sack as tight as she could and drew her sword. Then with the hilt began beating the bag over and over. From inside the sack came the demons shrill voices threatening her with vengeance and cruel revenge. So she picked the sack up and swung it above her head, striking it against the palace walls. Eventually, the demons began to stop their threats and instead began beseeching the Eldest Sister to stop their torture, promising that they would leave the kingdom and never return. The Eldest Sister knew, however, to not idly take the word of a demon, so as she loosened the sack to release her hostages she took a jewel from the top of the loudest demon's crown. She declared that she would keep the jewel as proof of the contract between them. This forced the demons to keep their word, but also tied the loud demon to her, forcing it under her command. Should she ever need its help the demon would have to appear by her side and do her bidding. The demon was shocked and embarrassed by this forced contract, but all the other demons so desperately wanted to leave the sack that it agreed to the terms. The Eldest Sister loosened the knot of the sack completely and released the horde of demons, who quickly exited the palace and the kingdom, kept to their word, and never returned.

As the light of the morning sun crept through the palace's stained glass windows, the Youngest Sister and her husband, the Mahārāja, opened the grand doors and burst into the great hall, panicked and terrified at what gruesome scene they might find. But instead of the peril they expected, they found the Eldest Sister smiling and sitting alone. The Youngest Sister was quick to embrace her sister, overcome with joy that she was safe and unharmed. The Eldest Sister explained her night's escapades, and how the kingdom was now safe from the tyranny of the demons. News soon spread of her courageous and ingenious accomplishment, and the whole kingdom erupted in celebration of the peace and happiness she had achieved for everyone.

Good fortune reigned over the kingdom and its people for many years. The Eldest Sister was content in her part of this peace, her battle wounds completely healed, and she had no more demons to fight. But despite all of this she wasn't happy. She didn't allow others to suspect this either, always putting on a brave and joyous facade especially in front of her Youngest Sister so as not to concern her. However, her lonley fate changed one day whilst she was browsing the local market stalls, from across the uniform pyramids of spices came an irresistible sweet smell. The Eldest Sister was quick to manoeuvre through the crowds of shoppers to follow this tantalising smell.

Attracted by the kind of intoxicating trance that brings a butterfly to nectar, this sweet and addictive fragrance is how the Eldest Sister found her soulmate. At the edge of the market, stood a tall woman selling many flavoured laddus, a sphere-shaped sweet the Eldest Sister had become fond of since her time living in this new kingdom. However, her fondness of the confectionary was now overshadowed by her growing attraction for the women selling them. Dark hair framed a heart-shaped face, expressive eyes bright with humour glanced towards her. And at the moment their eyes met they felt the depth, length and importance of their entire relationship all at once before it had even begun. Overwhelmed by emotions that didn't seem to make any sense, this was the instance they would later realise that they had fallen in love with each other, and with this love, the Eldest Sister had now found happiness. But alas this happiness and peaceful life weren't too last.

After years of uninterrupted happiness together, a cruel and relentless fever befell the Eldest Sister's partner. No doctor or healer could cure the disease, all they could offer the Eldest Sister was their condolences. It was when the doctors with their shaking heads stopped visiting and instead men with wood for a pyre stood outside their home that the Eldest Sister realised that she had to do something herself. Then with no other plausible options in front of her, she remembered the contract she had formed with the loud demon in the palace's grand hall. Holding the jewel she had taken from the demon's crown she desperately called out for the demon to appear and listen to her command.

A gust of icy wind blew through their humble home, slamming all the doors and windows that dared try and stop it open. In a puff of smoke and flash of light, her demon appeared before her, sarcastically bowing on one knee. But she did not have time for its games or jokes and quickly explained about the incurable illness her love had contracted, begging and demanding that the demon give her a remedy. She so desperately wanted a cure that she even began promising the demon it's freedom if he could remedy the disease and save her partner's life.

The demon was unexpectedly taken aback by this panic, the master they remembered was calm and collected even in the face of their own death. But here was a chance for the demon to regain their freedom, so it presented the Eldest Sister with an intricate glass chalice. The demon explained that for their freedom they would gift the Eldest Sister this enchanted chalice. Once the chalice has been filled with cold water and placed over the head of anyone who is bedridden, you can then look within the water's reflection and see Death. Without hesitation, the Eldest Sister filled the chalice with water and looked into the glistening reflection.

What the Eldest Sister saw was not the grotesque fearsome monster she had expected Death to be. Instead, she saw a human-like figure with a kind smile and mischievous eyes. They wore whimsical clothes that were adorned with bags of dazzling marbles. She was confused as to why Death would carry so many children's marbles. Her demon revealed that each marble was a soul that Death had collected. The more colours the marble had the more lives the soul had lived. But the Eldest Sister remained confused and agitated, she sharply barked at her demon asking how would seeing Death help her save her partner's life or was the demon just mocking her with the inevitable? The demon scoffed at her lack of faith in them, demons may be tricksters but you should never doubt their commitment to a contract. And they would never dare ignore a command given from a contracted master. Now slightly irritated at being so rudely disrespected, the demon begrudgingly explained that it was seeing where Death stood in the reflection that mattered. For if Death stands by the head of the bed of the ailed then they will not live to see another day, for Death was ready to take their soul, and not even a demon's power can prevent this.

However, this was not what they saw in the water's reflection, instead, Death was perched menacingly at the foot of the bed. The demon, with its mischievous smirk, took some of the water from the chalice and sprinkled it over the Eldest Sister's sick partner. As soon as the water droplets touched her soft dark skin, the miraculous happened, she opened her eyes and sat up smiling brightly. The overjoyed Eldest Sister wrapped her arms lovingly around her in a gentle embrace. For the demon's trick had worked, her partner was now completely cured of all that ailed her. The demon was quick to snatch his jewel from his once masters hand, and placed it back on top of his crown. Now the contract was done the demon with a wink and a smile vanished from the Eldest Sister side, never to be called upon again.

With the enchanted chalice in one hand and her partner's hand in the other, the Eldest Sister was now able to travel the world as a famed healer. She would be invited into the homes of the bedridden, those who could not be cured by conventional medicine. Then by using the demon's chalice, she would know instantly who would die and who she could help recover. It did not matter to her if the ill was rich or poor, nor did it concern her what faith or race they were. She always did everything in her power to help whoever was in need. This unwavering kindness meant that even if she arrived too late to help someone the family would thank her all the same, for at least she had tried to save their loved one. She was living a blessed and prosperous life when she received an urgent message from her Youngest Sister.

The message explained that her Youngest Sister's husband the Mahārāja had suddenly been taken by a cruel fever and with it neighbouring enemies had begun to take advantage of his frail state bt positioning their troops on the country's borders. The letter continued that the entire kingdom desperately needed the Eldest Sister to return to the palace and cure him, as she had so many others. Without a seconds thought the Eldest Sister rushed back to her Youngest Sister's kingdom and upon arrival was quickly ushered into the royal palace and to the unconscious Mahārāja's bedside.

The Eldest Sister tentatively took out her magic chalice and with an unsteady hand began to fill it with water. The room was filled with austere officials and grumbling priests, all intently judging her every move, and at the centre of the room sat her Youngest Sister silently weeping over her husband's frail form. The Eldest Sister approached the bedside gesturing to her Youngest Sister with her eyes, despite their long time apart, right now there was no time for friendly greetings or warm embraces. She peered into the chalice's reflection, her nervous grip making small ripples in the water's surface. After a sharp and bitter exhale she saw what she dreaded the most. Death looming over the head of the bed ready to take the Mahārāja's soul.

After explaining that there was nothing she could do to save the Mahārāja's life, panic and anger filled the room. But none took the news harder the Mahārāja's wife. The news that her husband was destined for death shattered the heart of the Youngest Sister and left her filled with intense despair, that clouded her mind with a bitter rage. She was unable to understand how her Eldest Sister could heal strangers, beggers, and criminals so easily, but when she needed her the most she couldn't heal her own brother-in-law? Guilt festered in the Eldest Sister, fed by the harsh words of all that surrounded her, plus the sight of her Youngest Sister filled with such hopelessness only cemented her resolve. She needed to mend her Youngest Sister's broken heart, and the only way to do this caused the Eldest Sister to come to a frightful decision.

The problem was that when Death decides to take a soul there wasn't anything even the most powerful wizard could do, but the quick-witted Eldest Sister thought to herself, if she could not stop the taking of a soul, she could instead change which soul Death took. Now steadily gripping the enchanted chalice she peered deep into the water's reflection and whilst determinedly looking Death in the eyes, beseeched them to allow the Mahārāja to live and to instead take her soul. For she would rather die by her own decision than live and see her Youngest Sister heartbroken. Death knew full well the value of the Eldest Sister's soul, with the enchanted chalice she had prevented many from reaching the point of being so unwell that Death could take them to the afterlife.

After imploring Death so wholeheartedly the Eldest Sister watched through the glass as Death moved steadily from the head of the bed to standing next to the feet of the Mahārāja. She knew then that her offer had been accepted, and that Death would take her soul instead. Dipping her fingers in the water of the chalice, she sprinkled some over the Mahārāja. In an instant, he sat up and was completely recovered and healthy again. In awe, all around his bedside cheered and rejoiced at the miracle they had just witnessed. The Youngest Sister embraced her husband with joyous tears flowing down her face, her heart whole and filled with love again. However, due to all this celebration, no one noticed the Eldest Sister's suddenly pale face and frail body silently leave the royal palace and return to her own home and bed.

Now extremely weak, the Eldest Sister lay in her bed sick and dying, with her partner sobbing next to her side. Just before she took her last breath she used what little strength she had left and looked into the water-filled chalice's reflection. And as expected saw Death sat next to her at the head of the bed, with a lamentable gaze. But the cunning Eldest Sister was not going to give up her soul so easily. From under her bedsheets, she pulled out the sack the wizard had gifted her many years before. She asked Death did they know what it was? Death intrigued replied that it was a sack. The Eldest Sister smirked and told Death that if it was a sack, then they should get into it!

Without argument or struggle, Death was pulled straight inside. The Eldest Sister quickly closed the sack and tied a tight knot around it. Instantaneously the illness that had so quickly struck her down disappeared just as fast. But she did not stop to celebrate, she had to ensure her plan continued to work. Hastily leaving her bewildered partner at home, she hurried as fast as her feet could carry her to the slumbrous forest. Then made her way through the brambles and tall grass to the densest part of the forest. Once she was sure no one had followed or seen her, she picked out the tallest tree, climbed to the top and on the highest branch hung the sack. And then promptly fell off the tree. But nothing quite cushions a fall than Death off duty. So alive and uninjured she returned home and swore to herself to never reveal to anyone else where she had hidden the sack.

Word that the great evil of Death had been trapped soon spread not only through the kingdom but all around the world. Celebrations and parties filled towns and streets, people from all walks of life brought together in rejoicing at the news that everyone and everything could no longer die. Immortality was now everyones, now they could all live with nothing to fear. At least this was how it was to begin with. Many years passed, people were born and kept on being born, and a curious realisation began to slowly creep into the minds of the now immortal.

On a rather cold winter's morning, the Eldest Sister peered out of her bedroom window and through the light mist of the morning saw spectres of what was once people. Empty shells of human figures wandering tirelessly through the streets, whose purpose in life had dwindled and now only existed due to the obligation of their forced immortality. They'd become so old that whichever way the wind blew they all inclined. For without Death the world and its people had been left in a peculiar limbo. Wars were being fought where no side could either win or lose any battles, armies at the end of a long day of combat would be exhausted and intact. Duals and executions would last full days and end with everyone rather confused. Star-crossed lovers would fling themselves off high cliffs, only to be left at the bottom a little sore and very embarrassed. These cursed souls were left waiting for Death's release, a release that would not come.

The Eldest Sister could not bear to live in a world filled with so much endless suffering any longer, especially knowing full well that she was the cause. With a heavy conscious she said her final farewells to all her loved ones, including her cherished Youngest Sister. Then she journeyed back to the slumbrous forest to retrieve the magical sack and release Death, thus taking her place in the afterlife. However, unbeknownst to the Eldest Sister, during the time trapped in the sack Death had grown to know fear. Fear of being captured and restrained, fear of being powerless, but most of all, Death had gained an intense fear of the Eldest Sister and her sack. So upon the sack opening, rather than finally taking the Eldest Sister's soul, Death instead fled as fast and as far away from the Eldest Sister as they could travel. Leaving her alone and alive.

Once Death was released back unto the world, mortality was restored. This allowed everyone to now live and enjoy their lives to the full, knowing any minute could be their last. Everyone that is except for the Eldest Sister. Death in their eternalness never for a moment forgot their fear of the Eldest Sister and the time spent imprisoned in the sack.

As the years continued on Death instead came for the souls of everyone close to the Eldest Sister. Gradually Death took the souls of everyone she loved, but never when she was present, which meant she was always unable to say her last goodbyes. Condemned to watch others age and die. Until one day when she was running a simple errand in the marketplace, whispers began to engulf the air, and with a deep sigh, she knew the loud commotion meant only one thing. Her Youngest Sister, the kingdom's ruler, had passed away. Death had finally collected her precious Youngest Sister's soul. A soul so bright that even Death paused to admire the beauty of the colours it emitted.

Now the Eldest Sister was completely alone and unable to join any of her loved ones in the afterlife. Instead, she was forced to live on and on and on until she could endure it no longer. In her youth, she had not let Death stop her from achieving her intentions, so if Death would not take her, she decided that she would just have to take herself to the afterlife. With the feared magical sack in one hand and the enchanted chalice in the other, the Eldest Sister dragged her dust and fragments to the edge of the Earth and then continued on further. After countless years of wandering, she discovered a way to the entrance of Hell that did not require Death's permission. But who should be guarding the gateway than the demons she had tricked so many years ago in the palace's great hall. Despite all the time that had passed they hadn't forgotten the magic sack and could still recognise the older and worn Eldest Sister.

The shrieks they let out in fear roused the infernal powers and they looked out from the unbreakable stone bridge. Go away! They fiercely commanded, petrified at the sight of her. The Eldest Sister fell to her aged knees and begged and pleaded with all the energy she had left after her long journey to be let into Hell, accepting that she would be tortured for her sins. But the demons would have none of it and ignored her sorrowful supplication. There was no way her or her sack were ever getting even one inch closer to the afterlife that she so greatly desired.

The venerable Eldest Sister knew that arguing with these demons was futile. Instead, she decided to appeal to their wily nature and tried to make a deal. If they would give her just one hundred souls they no longer had use of and a map to Heaven, then she would return to them the enchanted chalice that gave the user a glimpse of Death, and she would leave Hell and never return. Glad of any deal that removed the sack from their presence, the demons hastily agreed to her terms adding that they would give double the souls she asked for if she left instantaneously. Contract agreed the devils promptly rounded up what was required, gifting the Eldest Sister two hundred souls and a map to Heaven. The Eldest Sister gathered up the souls in her sack and the demons hurriedly escorted her out of Hell.

Without stopping to catch her breath she used the map and trudged onward to the entrance of Heaven. Her plan was simple, by returning these tortured souls to Heaven her sins would be pardoned and she too would be granted entrance. However, upon her arrival at the miraculous gates of Heaven, she was met with more disappointment. For the guardians of Heaven would only allow the two hundred souls she had brought to enter. The angelic guardians in unison and with calm dignified expressions explained that the Eldest Sister had not yet had her soul released from her mortal body by Death, and therefore would never be granted entrance. But the Eldest Sister was just as quick-witted and cunning as she had been in her youth.

With an understanding nod, she loosened the knot around the enchanted sack and released the two hundred souls. The mighty guardians opened the imposing gates and began to allow the liberated souls one by one into Heaven. All the Eldest Sister could do is watch as others she had saved were granted redemption. This was until the final soul was about to enter Heaven. Just as the last soul was about to pass through the gates, she discreetly passed them her magical sack, whispering the instructions that once inside Heaven they need to call her into the sack.

Of course the soul agreed to this plan, the Eldest Sister had saved them from the fiery pits of Hell and eternal torture, then delivered them to Heaven. The great gates closed behind the final soul and the guardians began a timeless slumber. The soul entered Heaven with the sack in hand ready to repay the Eldest Sister's kindness, and the Eldest Sister stood moments away from paradise waiting to be called in.

The Eldest Sister waited, and waited and waited some more, but despite listening intently, no invitation or call came for her. For what she didn't know was that there is no memory in Heaven, when a soul enters they forget everything that they once knew. So the soul with the sack had forgotten her and all that they had talked about moments after entering. Thus the Eldest Sister was left behind moments from paradise, she could not find a home in either Heaven or Hell, instead, she had to go on living in the world of mortals.

But do not be mournful for our friend the Eldest Sister, although now ancient with silver hair and sore bones, unlike the souls in Heaven she will never forget the joyous lifetime she had with her Youngest Sister, and all her loved ones, filled with such undying love and happiness. Now with the experience of age and a wily wit, she had remained just as smart and as cunning as she ever was in her youth.

The Eldest Sister resolved to live on with a purpose. Knowing Death would never appear when she was around she travelled the world visiting those moments from death and sat with them a while so that they could say their goodbyes and put any demons to rest. Allowing them to pass on with no regrets. For even to this day, when someone is in need of a little more time, quietly she will appear and grant them peace before they enter the afterlife. And then contently continue on in her neverending journey.

THE END.

EPILOGUE

This story was inspired by a Russian folktale originally called The Soldier And Death. In the original version of the story, a male soldier back from a twenty-year war helps his Slavic kingdom's Tsar. After which the Tsar becomes the soldier's benefactor but then falls ill, making the soldier obliged to save him. This was easily my favourite childhood story. Obviously, this is where I should tell you about my kooky Slavic grandmother who spoke very little English, smelt of lavender, and always had a bottle of vodka to hand. Who would often sit me down on her knee next to a roaring fire and tell me enchanting tales from her homeland. But sadly I don't have such a whimsical backstory of how this folktale became such a favourite of mine. Instead, I learnt about this story simply from sitting in front of a television watching a show created by the brilliant Jim Henson called The Storytellers.

As Jim Henson had already retold the original story so well I wanted to create my version of the tale in a completely different setting and with a more in-depth adventure and characters. So to mix it up I placed the story in Asia and had endless fun researching and incorporating Asian mythology and traditions, from the creatures that trouble the protagonist to the royal ceremonies, clothes, and customs. I hope you have enjoyed reading my first ever attempt at creating a storybook. Hopefully, the future will give me the opportunity to create even more stories filled with quirky characters and daring adventures for you to enjoy.

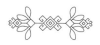

ABOUT THE AUTHOR

The artist Nona was born and resides in the city of Liverpool in the UK. Graduating from University with a Bachelor of Science in Computer Engineering. A self-taught artist, she has since had the pleasure of working on several illustration projects. From designing for the Burj Khalifa, to being exhibited at Hamlet's Castle in Denmark. She now tries to commit as much of her time to ongoing personal projects and storybooks.

Passionate about traditional art she has had work exhibited and sold across Europe, North America and Australia, and currently has a painting on permanent display at the Bluecoat Chambers in Liverpool. With a love for art, technology, and travel, Nona currently fits her drawing and painting around her day job and home life, with the hope that one day her passion for creating art and stories will become her full-time career.

Social Media: @nonaGalleryArt
Website: www.nonaGallery.com

ALSO AVAILABLE FROM NONA

HOROSCOPE WITCHES

Tap Into The Magic All Around You With Horoscope Witches, An Illustrated Guide To The Zodiac Signs As Witch Personas! A fascinating and wonderfully readable exploration of witchcraft, astrology, and character design. This comprehensive compendium is also a delightful page-turner that's full of unexpected treasures. Find out what magical abilities your date of birth deems you capable of!

MODERN MONSTERS

An A to Z anthology that travels the entire world meeting unusual and unique creatures from different mythologies. Exploring what these ancient beings are up to in the 21st century. From binging Netflix to enjoying Karaoke. Come join the adventure and follow the project as it unfolds for free online!

ARTIST - ILLUSTRATOR - AUTHOR
www.nonaGallery.com

@nonaGalleryArt